Little School

by Beth Norling

Kane/Miller
BOOK PUBLISHERS

for my little lion Indigo . who's about to start little school. love Mummy

First American Edition 2003
by Kane/Miller Book Publishers
La Jolla, California

First published by Omnibus Books,
a division of Scholastic Australia Pty Limited in 2001.
This edition published under license from Scholastic Australia Pty Limited.

Library of Congress Control Number: 2002112323

Printed and Bound in Singapore by Tien Wah Press (Pte) Ltd.

2 3 4 5 6 7 8 9 10

ISBN 1-929132-42-5

Thank you to Penny for her help with the words, Patricia for her help
with the design, and Dyan for having the idea for the book
in the first place!

Good morning – what a lovely day!
Wake up, everyone!

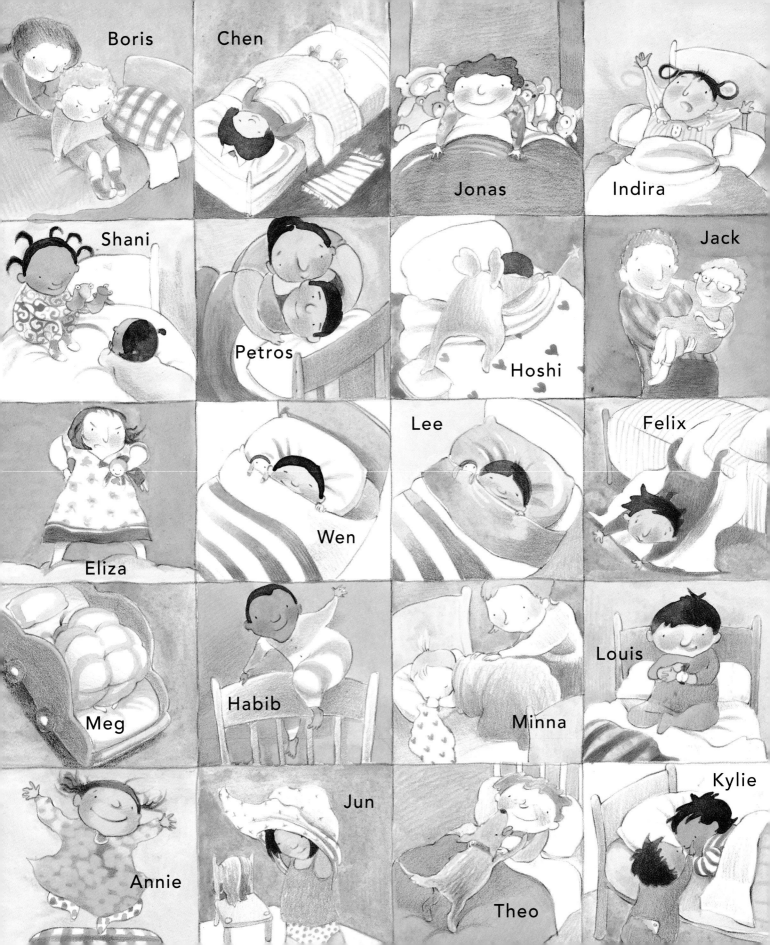

Boris

Chen

Jonas

Indira

Shani

Petros

Hoshi

Jack

Lee

Felix

Eliza

Wen

Meg

Habib

Minna

Louis

Annie

Jun

Theo

Kylie

Today we are all going to Little School.

Is everyone ready? Off we go!

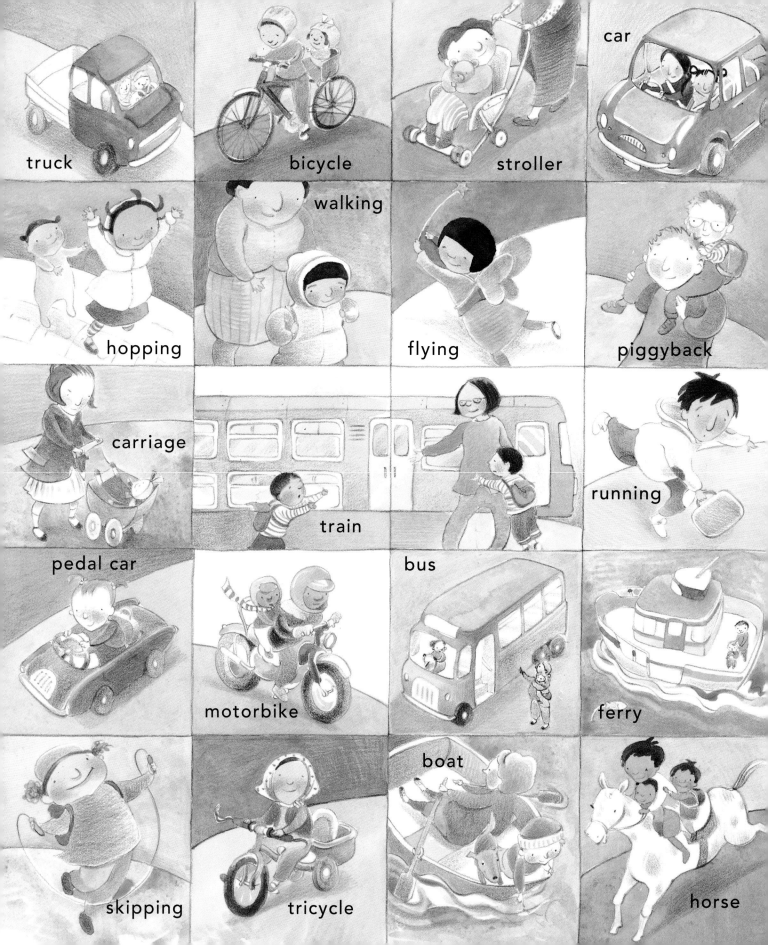

truck

bicycle

stroller

car

hopping

walking

flying

piggyback

carriage

train

running

pedal car

bus

motorbike

ferry

skipping

tricycle

boat

horse

Here we are at Little School.

Eliza puts her bag in the cubby.
Jonas takes off his coat.

We say goodbye to our families.

Come and see what's in our classroom!

tables

chairs

first-aid kit

easel

artwork

pets

bathroom door

paint smocks

sink

bulletin board

dress-up box

craft cart

computer

cushions

toys

piano

play kitchen

shelves

book rack

bins

Suzi and Jane and Ben are our teachers.
Jane has hair just like Shani's.

We love our morning song.
Jack sings the loudest.
We make lots of noise.

What's next? Let's make something!

clay

scissors

rolling pin

glue

crayons

paint brushes

pencils

paint

tape

paper

We go to the toilet and wash
our hands by ourselves.

We all sit down together
to eat our morning snack.

When we have finished,
we can choose a game!

felt farm
animals

building blocks

computer

magnetic
alphabet

nail board

number stencils

jigsaw puzzle

shapes

beads

dominoes

Oh dear, somebody isn't happy.

What do *you* have for lunch?

Shh! It's quiet time.

Kylie has chosen a book for Jane to read to us.
After our story, we go outside to play.

trampoline

balance
beam

see-saw

sand box

tunnel

jungle gym

slide

balls

big blocks

rocker

playhouse

We plant seeds at the nature table,
and water them to make them grow.

Louis, Annie and Chen make some
yummy biscuits.

Let's play again!

play
shop

playhouse

dress-up box

tea set

dolls

train

play dough

car

truck

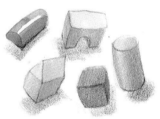
wooden blocks

Noah's ark

It's time to pack away the toys now.
Boris isn't helping at all.

Our families are here already.
What a busy day it's been!

Home again!
We still have lots to do before
we jump into bed.

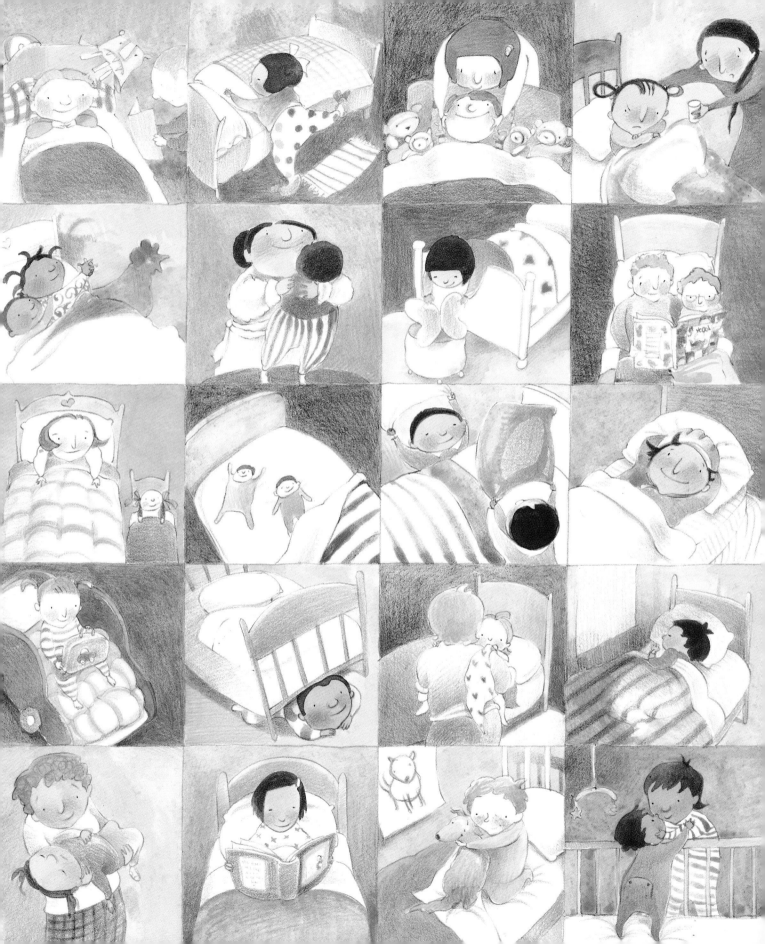

Goodnight! Sleep tight!